Savonne, Not Vonny

Savonne, Not Vonny

Robin Lee Lovelace

Etchings Press
Indianapolis, Indiana

This publication is made possible by the funding provided by the Shaheen College of Arts and Sciences and the English Department at the University of Indianapolis. Special thanks to IngramSpark and to those students who judged, edited, designed, and published this chapbook: Riley Childers, Shannon Harris, and Shauna Sartoris.

UNIVERSITY *of*
INDIANAPOLIS.

Published by Etchings Press
1400 E. Hanna Ave.
Indianapolis, IN 46227
All rights reserved

etchings.uindy.edu
www.uindy.edu/cas/english

Printed by Ingram
www.ingramspark.com

Published in the United States of America

978-0-9988976-9-1

Second printing, June 2021
23 22 21 20 19 2 3 4 5 6

Modified snake image on cover attributed to The Wildlife Center of Virginia.
Author photo by Jeff Lovelace.

My drops of tears I'll turn into sparks of fire.
-Shakespeare, *Henry VIII*

In 1967, a colony of bats took up residence in the abandoned building next to Mama Gwen's whorehouse down on the boulevard. On the northside of Indianapolis, not far from Crown Hill Cemetery. Mama Gwen's nine-year old granddaughter, Savonne, had a room in the back of the whorehouse, far away from the paying customers. Savonne was a working girl's baby, fathered by Mama Gwen's son Vic, who served as doorman, enforcer, money collector, and bartender. Savonne's mother was Coco Dupree: a half-creole girl who was the prettiest of the six whores working at Mama Gwen's house of ill repute.

Vic didn't question that he was Savonne's father because Savonne's skin was the same chocolate milk color as Vic's, and she was thin like him, tall like him, and had the same good teeth. Savonne was pretty, too. She had red-brown hair, full of crazy curls, and eyes the color of burnt sugar. Same color as Mama Gwen's, who she called Granny.

Savonne was soft spoken and quiet, but her mama, Coco, was a loud, crazy-ass woman who had a temper as hot as a Mississippi afternoon and she wasn't opposed to beating the shit out of somebody, if she got mad enough. One time she took a straight razor and sliced off the earlobe of a customer cause he called her a nigger. Another time she beat up a girl who was flirting way too much with Vic. She held the girl down with a knee to the neck and pulled out a tuft of the girl's hair. She threw it at Vic.

"Here you go, honey," she said. "You want her so bad. Have a piece."

Mama Gwen put up with crazy Coco Dupree cause Vic truly loved her. Even when Coco took a knife and ripped up the inside of his red Chevrolet when she got jealous one time, even when she threatened to cut off his man parts, even after she said she hated him, even after all that, Vic still loved Coco. So, every time something crazy happened, Vic would let it go because he had feelings for her. And Mama Gwen would let it go for a totally different reason. Coco was a hard worker and her best money maker. Why kick out the money?

Yes, and she adored her granddaughter. Mama Gwen had an abortion when she was younger, from a hacksaw up in Stringtown who said she had nurse training but all she did was mop hospital floors. Mama Gwen almost died and had to stay up in County General for four days and was made sterile from that hacksaw's butchery. Mama Gwen had sorrows about that. This was two years after she gave birth to Vic, her only son. When she got older and was making big money, Mama Gwen wished she had a daughter too. Couldn't have no more babies though, so Savonne was Mama Gwen's most precious little girl, more like a daughter than a granddaughter.

Some nights, Savonne would lay awake at night, in her bed, her wild hair haloed around her face, listening to the sounds of Motown music as it mixed with the laughter of the greasy-legged girls who worked the six downstairs bedrooms at Mama Gwen's.

That night, the first of July, the temperature went up to ninety degrees. Savonne's room got way too hot. Mama Gwen brought in an electric fan that made loud motorized noises that drowned out most other sounds.

"Savonne," she said over the racket. "Raise up the window, let some breathin air in here. Chile, you sweat to death without no breathin air."

Savonne raised the screenless window and propped it up with a splintery stick. Too high for street heat, the night air blew cool into the room, caught in the fan, and poured over Savonne like sprayed water

"Go on to sleep, now."

Mama Gwen left Savonne to the darkness.

Next door, a young bat walked across the floor of the empty building that stood only twenty yards away. Restless, the bat took wing, did a figure eight around the two buildings, and flew through Savonne's open window.

Still awake, Savonne watched the bat fly over her. At first, she thought it was just a bird. She froze up when she saw it was a bat, because she learned from TV that bats suck blood from people's necks. The bat circled the room, flapping its wings, trapped, until Savonne got brave enough to jump out of bed and run down to the parlor.

"Granny," she said, "Granny, they a bat in my room."

Mama Gwen smiled at a young john named Speedy and said, "Wait a min, honey," fetched her broom and followed Savonne upstairs. She swung and cut the broom through the air until the bat found its way out the window. Mama Gwen turned to Savonne.

"Baby, you alright?"

Wide eyed, she could only shake her head. Mama Gwen smiled.

"That bat weren't after you, it just got stuck and didn't know how to get out."

She patted Savonne's shoulder. "Let's close the window a little bit."

Mama Gwen took out the stick, let the window come down, and tucked the stick catty-corned against the windowsill.

"No bat get in here now," Mama Gwen declared to her granddaughter.

"Go on to sleep, now."

Mama Gwen headed back to her business, closing the door behind her.

Savonne went to her dresser, opened the top drawer, fished through candy wrappers and crayons until she found the little silver cross necklace Mama Gwen gave her for her ninth birthday. She put the cross around her neck, went back to bed, and held her hand over the crucifix until she fell into sleep. Later that night, outside Savonne's window, rain fell like stardust.

When Savonne woke the next morning, most of Mama Gwen's girls were already out shopping or gone home to their kids or counting money out to Vic.

Savonne ran down to the empty kitchen and got out a carton of milk, the sugar can, the Cheerios, and a big bowl. She poured milk and sugar in almost equal amounts over the O's until they floated in a sea of milk above mounds of sugar dunes.

With milk and mushy cereal sloshing in her stomach, Savonne grabbed her hula-hoop, jumped down the porch steps, and ran through the crooked gate. She practiced her hula-hoop tricks. Rainwater from the house's clogged gutters dripped in time to the swish of the hula-hoop. From an upstairs window, Aretha Franklin wailed about respect. Mama Gwen sang along, louder but just as soul-felt. The sun made everything look gold.

"What you doin?"

Savonne didn't look up. From the corner of her eye, she could see Tina's dirty red Keds at the end of her fat baby doll legs. Tina had a scab on one knee and a Band-

Aid on the other. Her cutoffs were fringed with loose white threads that hung down and tickled her skin, causing her to raise one knee to scratch every now and again. Tina lived four houses down, but she always came over to bother Savonne.

"Hula-hoop."

"I can do that."

"Can't."

"Better than you."

"Shut up." Savonne always told Tina to shut up whenever she tried to brag about herself.

"Savonne. Look what I got."

Tina held out a quarter.

"Mama give me this for being good and helpin with the dishes."

Savonne stopped her hula-hoop and squinted at Tina.

"So."

"So I'm goin to the store, wanna go too?"

"I ain't walkin to no store with you. You too stuck up."

"I ain't stuck up. You stuck up. Mama say you a whore's baby. Daddy say hard tellin if Vic is your real daddy, cause your mama lay-up with all sorts of men."

Tina pointed a finger in Savonne's face.

"Daddy say men give Mama Gwen money so they can rake them girls livin with you."

Savonne got a picture in her head of a man running a big metal rake over the girls while Mama Gwen sit in the kitchen counting money.

Later, Savonne walked to the store without Tina. Mama Gwen sent her for toilet paper and she got to keep the change from fifty cents.

The fat old white lady that owned the store was

sweeping the front sidewalk; the daughter, a fatter duplicate of her mother, waited on Savonne. After she paid for the toilet paper she only had a nickel, five cents shy of the cost of strawberry on a cone.

"I can sweep for you."

Savonne was hoping she could earn enough to make up the difference. The woman shrugged and handed her the broom.

Savonne set her bag of toilet paper up against the storefront and went to work. After a few minutes, the sidewalk was clear and clean. Savonne took the broom inside to the lady, who was now sitting behind the counter sanding down her nails.

"I finished," Savonne said with hope in her voice.

The woman took the broom from her, put it in the corner, and went to working on her nails again, ignoring Savonne.

Savonne picked up her package and walked home.

*

"Did you tell that old hag you wanted money before you start?" her daddy said, after he listened to her story.

Savonne shook her head.

"Then she didn't have to pay," Vic said. "You always ask what you gonna get before you do the work, or you get stung every time."

Savonne bowed her head, embarrassed about getting cheated.

"How much you need for your ice cream?"

"Nickel."

Vic stood up and went into his pocket. He held out a

handful of change. Savonne picked out a quarter.

"Thanks, Daddy."

He smoothed his palm over Savonne's crazy hair and her cheek. He smiled down at her.

"You welcome, baby girl. When you get back, you can do some sweeping for me."

"Yes, Daddy."

By the time Savonne got home, she had eaten most of the ice cream, but the sun melted some of it over her hand and her blouse.

Savonne saw her daddy come out of Mama Gwen's and sprint across the street to where he parked his car. Coco was with him. She ran far behind him, slower because she wore high heeled boots. Coco was Savonne's birth mother, but she didn't pay her no mind.

"Vic," Coco shouted, stranded in the middle of the street, waiting for a bus to pass. Vic, already across, motioned for her to come. Laughing, she ran into his arms and acted like she was fainting.

"Did you see?" Coco's voice was breathless and high-pitched. "Did you see the bus almost run over me? I swear, baby, I'm gonna get killed runnin after you."

Coco wore bright green eyeshadow and thick eyeliner that was drawn on very straight and extended way past her eyelids. Savonne thought it made her mama look like a cat.

She yelled to Savonne.

"What you got all over you, Vonny?"

"Strawberry."

Coco made a face.

Vic laughed. "Go on in the house, Savonne. Tell your granny to change your clothes."

Coco pulled at Vic's sleeve.

"Vic, buy me some ice cream," she said. "You can lick it off if it gets on my shirt."

"Yeah, what's Mama chargin your tricks to lick off ice cream?"

Coco screamed with laughter and lightly slapped Vic's chest.

"Vic, you too bold."

Savonne went through the gate and walked up the steps. She went into the house. The rest of the day curled away like smoke.

After supper, Savonne went to her room. She colored in her coloring book and listened to 45s on her red and blue record player. Savonne could do a lot of dances. She did the twist, the mashed potato, the swim, and the monkey, just like they did it on the television. Then Mama Gwen come upstairs to her room, handed her pajamas to her, and told her it was time for bed. Mama Gwen brushed oil into Savonne's wild hair and pulled it to the top of her head into a bushy ponytail.

Mama Gwen opened the window just a few inches, switched on the fan, and wished her granddaughter a good night. After Mama Gwen shut the bedroom door behind her, Savonne went to the dresser, got her necklace with the cross, and went back to her bed. She held the cross closed in her hand and prayed no bats would get in that night. Finally, Savonne fell to sleep.

*

Savonne saw a big, black tornado, wild, spinning closer until it was right outside her window. Inside the tornado, thousands of squeaking bats flew in circles, around and around. Somebody was shouting from the center of the tornado.

"Vonny, wake up."

It was Coco. She tapped Savonne on her cheek a few times until Savonne opened her eyes.

"Wake up. We got to go."

"What?"

"We goin. Right now."

"Where we goin?"

"Away from this awful place."

"Is Daddy goin too?"

"No, now get up. I got your clothes already. We leavin right now."

"Where's Daddy? Where's Granny?"

"Forget about them. We got to go. Come on."

Savonne got out of bed. She saw it was still dark outside her window.

"I want Daddy to go."

"Here's your shoes."

Savonne pulled on her tennis shoes.

"Take you clothes."

Coco handed Savonne a brown paper bag filled with clothes.

"Why we goin now? It's still dark."

"Be quiet.

"I don't want—"

"You need to shut up and be quiet, Vonny." Coco smacked Savonne on the back of her head. "Don't make me have to whup you."

Coco grabbed Savonne's hand and pulled her out of the bedroom and down the stairs to the dark, empty kitchen. It was long past closing time, almost morning, so she had to rush.

Coco went into the refrigerator, grabbed out a half-full bottle of vodka, put it in her big handbag, and pulled Savonne out the side door. They walked fast through the alley in the darkness until they got to Coco's beat up Volkswagon that was parked sideways, five houses down, next to somebody's back yard.

"Get in." Coco said in a whispery voice. "We goin to visit my Pappydad, down in Louisiana."

"When we comin back?" Savonne whispered.

"Don't know yet."

"Does Daddy know we leavin?"

"God dammit, stop talkin about your daddy."

Coco pushed Savonne into the passenger seat and quickly got in at the driver's side. Soon as Coco fished out her car keys, Savonne jumped out of the car and ran. Coco said, "Shit!" and ran after her, caught her by her arm, and pulled her back.

"What you think you doin?"

"I wanna stay with Daddy."

Coco pushed her into the Volkswagen.

"Your daddy is a no good, cheatin, lyin motherfucker," Coco said. "You ain't never goin to see him again. So shut up about it or I'll whup your ass."

Coco put the key in the ignition and started the car. She sucked in a big breath, let it out, wiped sudden tears from her eyes, and sniffed snot up into her nose so it wouldn't dribble out. She leaned her forehead on the steering wheel for a moment and said, "Everything's gonna be alright."

Coco's old VW lurched and clicked and rattled its

way through the bluegrass hills of Kentucky, over the blue mountains of Tennessee and the hot blacktop road through Alabama and into the muddy flatlands of Louisiana. Coco was taking Savonne to the only place she thought they'd never find her. Coco was taking the girl to stay with Pompey.

*

Pompey was a conjurer in his younger days, before he got caught up in the vodka bottle. He was pushing eighty and was reminded of it by the pain he felt in his joints, his dried-up feet, and from the rusted pain that never left him as it ran from behind his ear down the back of his skinny neck. Pompey had a perfectly round bald head that shined with a pink space of skin which was shaped like the map of Mother Africa.

Over the last few years his conjure ability went to weakness from lack of use. But he kept a gris-gris bag, graveyard dirt, and a bag of brick dust that he sprinkled at the doorway when he thought about it, and dried up chicken feet and the bleached jawbone of a swamp gator on his fireplace mantel. He still had possession of an ancient conjure book, inherited from the last true Voodoo Queen of the Caribbean who died in Natchez when Pompey was a young man. His only housemate was an old dog, once black haired, now gone to gray, who he called Leatha, named after his murdered girlfriend from nine years ago. Leatha was smart and told Pompey when people were coming to visit.

Pompey knew the dog was his Leatha, come back from the grave to trifle with him, laugh at him, and make him get bit with fleas that jumped from her body onto his bony feet. Pompey knew she'd come back to harass him because he was laid up drunk on the night that Leatha went into New Orleans and got herself cut up dead.

Leatha used to live with Pompey in the tin-roof house that sat in front of a field of junked cars and mounds of rubber tires. A sign on the fence in front of the house simply read 'Junkyard.' More like a graveyard. Pompey hadn't sold a tire, a steering wheel, or a transmission in three long years. Behind his shack, on down to the creek that ran at the edge of the property, was a half-mile field of dead cars and trucks. When it got cool in November, snakes would lie up in those cars, gathering the heat from the metal and the rubber. Wild dogs would walk among the cars and fight each other and bark at the moon on winter nights. Pompey was always scared the feral dogs would get his Leatha, and he hated the sound of the barking, so he'd throw a couple of shells in his shotgun and shoot above the cars until the dogs scattered and ran. Other nights, when he was drunk and thinking of Leatha, he would walk among the skeletons of the automobiles and try to whistle up some ghosts. Pompey lived on the government check he got in the mail every month and drank it up in vodka and went to corn liquor when his money got low. On the nights he was drunk on the corn was when he would go for the whistling walks.

The thing about Pompey was that he was not scared of man or nature. He lived his entire life like a fool, challenging men that he knew he couldn't whup, yelling sugar-coated words to women who wouldn't give him the time it takes to blink, teasing big dogs chained to rickety fence posts, and flipping off the police. Not scared of man, angel, or devil, except for one. That man would be Diamond John, who stood seven feet almost, was caramel colored, and wore his African hair lacquered and stiff as briar sticks. John had a diamond mounted in one of his front teeth that he would flash in the sun some days, when it wasn't gray skies or raining, and he had powerful tricks that he played out, so subtle and carefree that people didn't even know until some time later. John would turn an Ace into a Jack, cause a man to trip over a leaf and break his leg, make a woman to start bleeding even though it weren't her time of the month. Pompey didn't want to be John's Father-in-law, but he had no say in the matter. Pompey's own daughter, Neicey, went up and married Diamond John seven years ago, on the day before Easter, 1960.

Pompey knew John had the natural in him, and he was rightly wary of him. And Diamond John knew that Pompey had the natural too, and a conjure book full of pure, old time Caribbean spells that Pompey had secreted away somewhere in his rickety-ass house. Diamond John's mouth watered when he thought about getting his hands on that conjure book. He knew Pompey weren't even interested in gathering up ingredients or giving up some of himself to work the powerful spells in the book. Diamond John was interested, though, and willing to sacrifice for whatever the spells called for. Diamond John thought he should be the owner of the conjure book. He could put it to good use.

Sometimes Pompey thought John was the reason Leatha got cut up in New Orleans. Pompey didn't think it was John who did the cutting, but he thought John might've caused it with a spell that he used on Leatha. He thought this because one night, when they were all drunk and drinking, he got mad at Pompey for telling Leatha that John liked to put his thing in parts of women that it ought not to go. This happened a year before Diamond John jumped broom with Neicey.

Leatha laughed at John in her high, musical laugh and said John's thing was probably mighty stinky if he was putting it places it shouldn't go, and John rose up out of his chair and smacked Leatha across the face so hard that Leatha fell against the kitchen table. Pompey went into his bedroom quick as a jackrabbit and got his shotgun. He pointed both loaded barrels at John and told him it was time for him to get out of his house. John walked out to his flatbed truck, turned around, and waved his hand in a subtle way. Pompey saw what he was doing so he fired one barrel of rock salt at John, not to kill him but get his conjuring ways negated. John ducked and only the edge of the spray of rock salt caught him across his waist, leaving blood marks and ripped skin, but nothing close to fatal. John managed to get into the truck and drive himself home. The next day, John was still picking pebbles of salt out of his skin but none of it went in deep and it didn't do damage to his insides. Two weeks later, Leatha was sliced up in an alley next to a Hoodoo Club at the end of the French Quarter. Pompey imagined Diamond John sitting and smiling, looking down into his whiskey glass when a young man bust into the Club and yelled, "They a woman cut up dead in the alley."

Pompey went to where they laid out Leatha at the city morgue. Policemen said Leatha didn't even have time to turn around. Whoever or whatever cut her came up behind her, sliced her neck open, dragged her into the alley, sliced the veins in her arms at the crook, and cut her thigh open at the large leg vein. Blood poured out of her in pints and she must've died in less than a minute. Pompey called Leatha's sister, Alvena, up in Memphis and she came down on the train and helped Pompey arrange Leatha's funeral and wake.

Pompey laid Leatha down in her family's tomb in New Orleans. The next day, after Leatha's body was put into the dark, dry room of the tomb, a black dog with bright brown eyes came to Pompey's house and barked until Pompey opened the front door and let the mongrel in. It was Leatha come back with all her stubbornness and her big loving heart. He could tell in the easy way the dog cocked its head to the left when it heard something from far away, trying to listen, just like Leatha did in the days when Pompey had customers coming down the road.

Now Leatha was barking wildly, standing on the wooden porch, looking at something that was not showing its face just yet. Pompey opened the squeaky screen door and looked down the dirt road, which ran to a gravel road, which ran to a blacktop road, which ran into town.

Then Pompey saw a familiar flatbed truck rounding the corner. It had been years since he seen that black devil truck. Here come Diamond John. Big head behind the steering wheel, smiling that sparkling evil smile, hair still black as coal and slicked stiff with hair dip, looking steady straight at Pompey. Sitting next to John was Pompey's only daughter Neicey who was pushing fifty years old but still had a pretty face although her body had gone to fat shortly after she had passed into middle age. Neicey had a determined look on her face that baffled and unsettled Pompey. He hadn't seen Neicey in three or four years and now she was coming to his house, with Diamond John, and looking at him in a strange way. Something was about to happen, but Pompey didn't know just exactly what.

Pompey scattled into the house shouting conjure words of protection as he went to his bedroom and grabbed his shotgun that was already loaded up with metal buckshot. Pompey came back, quick as his old crimpy legs could go, with the shotgun pointed ahead of him. He threw the screen door open and aimed the gun steady at the driver's side of the truck that was now in the parking gear with engine idling, positioned directly in front of Pompey's front door. No one was behind the steering wheel, and Neicey was still sitting in the truck on the passenger side but had the cab door open. Pompey started to turn to the right when Diamond John's broad hand flashed out and grabbed the shotgun by the barrel before Pompey could swing it all the way round. Diamond John jerked the gun out of Pompey's hands.

"Not today old man," Diamond John said and broke the gun open, took out the shells and threw them into the tall grass that Pompey kept telling himself he would get around to mowing one day.

From the cab of the truck, Neicey yelled to Pompey.

"Come to tell you somethin."

"Tell me what?" Pompey yelled, still watching Diamond John, wary and waiting for any sign of spell making.

"Coco comin back. Comin to see ya," Neicey yelled.

"What?"

Pompey hadn't seen his granddaughter Coco since Leatha's funeral. Coco weren't no more than seventeen or eighteen years old. Still in school and living with her mother.

"She done something bad up north. She bringin her child to you. For you to watch for a while until she figures out what to do about it."

"What?"

"You heard me, you sorry old fool. Coco be here tonight. Be ready. Don't be drunked up either." Neicey got out of the truck and took a couple steps closer.

"What Coco do?" Pompey yelled.

"Don't know," Neicey said, walking closer.

"Why she bringin a child out here? To me?"

"Cause you Coco's Grandaddy or do you forget that fact?" Neicey said. "Cause she trusts you. Cause she a granddaughter of a fool and she a lot like her Granddaddy."

Pompey saw Diamond John break out a smile again. His big, donkey teeth spread over the bottom half of his face like a Chessy cat. The diamond imbedded in his tooth sparkled under the midday sun.

"I can't take care no child. I ain't no babysitter."

Pompey watched Diamond John for a hand movement or a whispered spell.

"You been told," Neicey said.

"Neicey, you can take care of it better'n me," Pompey said.

Neicey stepped a few feet closer to Pompey.

"Why don't you get a phone out here?"

"Can't afford it."

"You can afford a bottle of vodka every day, but you can't afford a telephone?"

"I can't take care of no child," Pompey declared.

"Yes you can. If you stop that drinkin. Took care of me, didn't you?"

"Your mama took care of you, mostly," Pompey

answered. "Neicey, you a mama, too. You should be the one."

"I can't do it. I got business to attend to. I ain't raisin another child. Didn't do too well with the first one."

"Why don't Coco just take care of the child herself?"

"Ask her that when she get here."

"You still got that book, old man?" Diamond John interrupted. "That conjure book you stole from that witch up in Natchez?"

"I still got that book, but I ain't never stole it. It was given to me and it is rightfully mine, and you ain't never gonna see it."

"Don't need no book, old man. Never did."

"Why you ask me about it every time I see you? You ain't been up in these parts for eight or nine years now and still you askin bout that conjure book."

Neicey waved goodbye with a flick of her hand, walked to the truck, and stepped up into the cab.

Diamond John followed, hopped up into the driver's side, pulled the truck in reverse, backed up, then circled around. He stepped heavy on the gas and took off, kicking up dirt and grass.

"I'll be Goddamned and the Baptist on a silver plate." Pompey swore like that, like no other person swore. Putting words together that didn't sound quite right but were un-mistakenly meant as swear words.

Last Pompey heard, Coco went up to Chicago, then went to Indianapolis, where she made her money by spreading her legs. His own granddaughter, Coco. Making her living as a goddamn mattress. He blamed Niecey for his granddaughter's waywardness. Hell cook in the damn fire, he wasn't around Coco enough to influence her. She left New Orleans as soon as she had enough money to buy a car.

And Diamond John made sure nobody was that close to Coco's mother, Neicey, except himself. And Pompey could see why. She was still a pretty woman even in her middle age with her auburn hair pinned up in a beehive and with her smooth skin, and she could cook like God's own Angels. Pompey taught her that. Good enough to open a barbeque pit on Terpsichore Street and made a nice living serving up ribs and chicken. Famous for her corn pudding. Had a good mind for business too. Open the ribs place, bought a Laundromat, made that into a moneymaker, and even helped Diamond John run his Voodoo shop on Broad Street.

Pompey was sure that it was Neicey that kept his old skinny ass alive. John wouldn't do a thing to make Neicey hate him, and killing her daddy would be the worst thing he could do. Even through conjures, Neicey would be suspicious. She was perpetually mad at Pompey for drinking his life away, for leaving her mother and taking up with Leatha, for letting the junkyard rust into nothing, but she would be more than mad at Diamond John if he caused Pompey any harm.

Now what Coco gone and done? Something bad. And she have a kid?

Pompey stepped off the porch and went into the tall grass to find the shotgun shells that Diamond John tossed away. He found one quick but never did find the other and had to give up on looking. Pompey stepped close to a snake that was living in the grasses, and the snake slithered away before Pompey even knew it was there.

*

It was the time of day when the sky is just dark enough to reveal the moon. Leatha stood up slowly, went to the front door, and waited. Pompey was dozing in his easy chair, TV set on low. A couple minutes went by, and Leatha started a growl in her throat that exploded into a mess of barks. She was old for a dog, almost gone all to gray, stiff boned, but steadfast in her ability to smell and sense what was coming down the road for Pompey.

It was Coco. Rounding the bend, tired, smelling of Salems and french fries, wearing a dirty T-shirt, a pair of cut-offs, and a red scarf tied round her head, riding her crumpled-up Volkswagen Beetle, scratched and dented with yellow paint scraped off in places, but puttering along. Savonne was sitting next to her, brown eyes wide and scared, long, crazy hair pulled back and rubber-banded in a ponytail, holding a bottle of Coca-Cola with both hands.

Pompey went to the front door, switched on the porch light, opened the screen door, and stepped out to watch and wait.

Coco slowed down, stopped, turned off the car engine, motioned to the girl to get out, and got out herself.

"Pappydad," Coco said quietly.

She never called him nothing but Pappydad all her life—never Grandpa or Granddaddy or even Pompey, always it was Pappydad as far back as he could remember.

"Coco, you a sight."

She went to him and they hugged for a long time. He felt tears forming in his old dry eyes. It surprised him.

After a while she pulled away and said, "I did somethin stupid."

"Heard you did. Your mother came up and told me."

Pompey turned his gaze to the brown-skinned girl that was now standing at the edge of the porch, still holding a half-full bottle of Coke.

"This your girl, huh?"

"Yeah. That her. She don't talk much."

"She don't? What's her name?"

"Vonny. I call her Vonny."

"My name is Savonne, not Vonny."

"How old is she?"

"Almost ten," Savonne said.

"You hungry…Savonne?" Pompey said.

Savonne put her hand over the cross she wore around her neck and silently asked God to let her go home. She didn't want to talk to this old man. They drive all day, and now they were at this rusted tin roof house that look just like the shack on the *Green Acres* television show.

Pompey looked at Coco. "She hungry?"

"Well if she ain't, I am," Coco answered. "What you got?"

"Baked rabbit and dressing that I cooked this morning when I thought you'd be here earlier. A little bit of greens from yesterday. Mac and cheese. Dirty rice. I brewed some tea and sliced a lemon up in it. And I gotta bag of ice in the cooler, probably done half melted by now."

Coco went into the house that was lit up with electric in two rooms and an oil lamp in the back bedroom.

On the kitchen counter was the pan of baked rabbit and corn bread dressing. Still smelling savory and fragrant.

Coco hadn't ate rabbit in a long time and the smell of it was like music. Her diet up north was mostly cheeseburgers and fries and the occasional chocolate bar. And a lot of vodka to get her through the nights of sucking dick and humping old white men. And cold drinks. Coco loved her some orange soda poured over big square ice cubes.

Coco said, "Where you keep the plates?" and Pompey pointed to the tin door cabinet. Coco went to it, opened the door, and grabbed her a plate, then another plate from the stack for the girl. Coco said to Savonne, "You want some rabbit and dressing?"

Savonne shook her head.

"If you hungry that's what you gonna get, if you want it or not. Now. You hungry?"

Savonne answered "Yes."

"Well then."

Coco dipped a big metal spoon into the rabbit dressing and plopped a mound of it on the plate.

Next to the rabbit was a pan of macaroni and cheese, and next to that was a bowl of collards. A pot of dirty rice filled with chunks of chicken livers, and Andouille sausage sat on the top of the stove.

"You want some of this too?" Coco pointed the metal spoon toward the pan of macaroni and cheese. Savonne said "Okay," and Coco put a big spoon of it on the plate, went to the pot of dirty rice, put a spoonful of the rice on the plate, and put some of the collards on the plate too. Some green liquid leaked out of the collards and bumped into the macaroni and cheese and even into the rabbit dressing. Savonne hoped it didn't make the food taste like the collards smelled, cause what it smelled like was vinegar and dandelions.

Coco put down a metal cup of watery ice, poured sweet tea over it and handed it to Savonne.

"Go take your plate out to the porch and eat your food," Coco ordered. "Me and Pappydad gotta talk."

Savonne did what she was told. She found a rocking chair and sat on the edge of it with her plate balanced on her lap. She ate in silence, in the dark, watching lightning bugs float though the air, blinking and winking to each other in some secret insect code. Tears came to her eyes and she wiped them with her hand. She wanted to go home.

The gray dog named Leatha found her and came trotting up from the yard. Leatha sat in front of the girl, watching and guarding Savonne, barking a single bark every few seconds to demand a bite of rabbit. Inside the house, Coco explained to Pompey why she took the girl.

"You did what?" Pompey said in a hushed voice. "You killed the girl's father?"

"I shouldn't done it. But he was in there fucking that new bitch, and me right in the house, working two bedrooms down. Getting paid measly-ass money while he up in there fucking another woman?"

Coco took a chunk of ice out of her cup and put it in her mouth. She crunched on the ice and gave Pompey a stubborn look.

"So I did a little sumthin to his shot glass."

"What you do?"

Coco smiled, the edges of her mouth curled up, but her eyes teared up a little. She moved her head away from Pompey.

"I use the goofer recipe," she whispered. "The one I learnt from your book."

Pompey sighed, wiped a hand over his bald head. He showed Coco the conjure book when she was twelve years old. He should have known it was knowledge he didn't need to give out to them that didn't have the natural. And never to them with evil in their hearts. Coco never showed signs she had the natural and somewhere along the way she'd picked up a dose of evil. Now she done used the most dangerous recipe in the book.

"You know how much time you get in prison for poisonin somebody to death?"

"Shit, they lucky I didn't poison all of em. I thought about it."

Coco took off her head scarf, scratched her scalp.

"You know what?" Coco said with a mouthful of spitefulness, "He said he loved me, Pappydad. He said he loved me. That's why I had his child. That's why I stay there so long. So why he couldn't keep his pants up?"

Pompey leaned in and in a low voice said, "You caused somebody to die. That ain't right. No matter the reason."

Coco wasn't listening. She was bringing it all out. She was steaming like hot water from a teapot.

"You should see the way he dote on Vonny. He spoilt her and bought her stuff she don't need and take her to the movies all the time."

"That don't give you the right to kill him."

Coco slammed the cup down on the table.

"That didn't give him the right to treat me like shit. I was his girl. And I brought in big money, while he was fuckin around on me. I am the mother of his child, and I didn't get a drip of respect from him. He say he loved me, but he treat me just like he treated all those other girls."

Pompey shook his head, scared for Coco. What

happened to her? What'd Neicey do wrong to turn out a child like this. A murderer? Coco always had a temper but Pompey woulda bet his last dollar bill that she'd never do something like this.

"The law gonna come for you. They gonna be down here lookin for you. And her. They gonna find you. More sooner than later."

"They ain't gonna know what happened. Them folks up North don't know about the conjure or Voodoo or root work."

"They gonna know a man was poisoned. They gonna know you gone right after he died."

Coco left that night before Savonne woke from her cot in the front room. Coco left the child with Pompey and never came back.

*

For two years, Savonne lived with Pompey. He never talked much to her about her mama or why Coco brought her to him. Savonne asked more than a dozen times, and Pompey would just tell her when she got older her mama would come for her. The first time she asked about her daddy, which was the day after Savonne was brought to him, Pompey told the girl that her daddy and mama got into an argument and her daddy had a heart attack and died. He didn't want to tell the child her mama killed her daddy. Poisoned him with Alumic rubbed over his shot glass and a half teaspoon of goofer mixed up in his whiskey bottle. The old-time recipe, straight from his conjure book. Savonne cried and laid on the cot for two days, mourning the loss of her daddy.

After Savonne got so sad, Pompey decided to teach the girl a little of the conjure to occupy her mind and get her to stop thinking about her dead daddy. He showed her how to make minnows jump into a coffee can, make butterflies light on her shoulder, make grass grow into flowers; only harmless little things like that. Pompey could tell she had the natural, inherited the gift from himself, but he never showed her the conjure book.

One starlit night, Savonne wanted to show Pompey a conjure she made up on her own. Pompey went to the porch, lit up a cigarette, and watched while Savonne walked out into the front yard. She raised her arms and held them high above her head. She spread her fingers apart and said five words:

Dife bestiola vin jwenn mwen

Lightning bugs quickly swarmed to her. They came out of the bushes and trees and flew above the tall grasses and weeds, straight to Savonne. They covered her hands like a pair of black gloves. Pompey never saw that before. The lightning bugs all flashed their lights at the same time, then flashed them once again and a third time. Savonne laughed and waved her hands. The lightning bugs flew off, launching a few at a time. They went straight back to where they came from. Savonne walked up the porch and stood in front of Pompey, rubbing her hands together. The lightning bugs made her skin tingle.

"What you think about that?" Savonne said.

"That a good conjure, Savonne. That a real good conjure."

It was clear then, to Pompey, that Savonne should own the conjure book. Not right now, though. Not on this day. A little girl with the natural as strong as that? With a powerful conjure book in her possession? That could make the world a dangerous place. And something could be hiding in her. Like in Coco. Something evil that he can't see quite yet. He needed to give it time, see what plays out. But Pompey couldn't deny. Savonne had the natural and had it strong.

"Where'd you find the words?" Pompey said.

"They come to me. I dreamed them."

Pompey went into the kitchen. He needed a drink.

*

The rest of the summer, Pompey kept busy teaching her skills she would need. How to fry chicken, catch mourning doves in a wire net, and where to find the good poke salad greens. Pompey made Savonne read the words she knew from the old books that Pompey kept on a wooden shelf in the television room. Pompey gave her numbers to cypher and showed her how to multiply and divide. Pompey sent the girl to Sally's grocery store when Pompey's check came in. Sometimes he let her buy a Coca-Cola or a candy bar or an ice-cream cup. When Christmas came, Pompey paid Sally from the store to drive him to the Goodwill. He bought Savonne a pair of tennis shoes and two pairs of jeans, a yellow, ruffled blouse with a tiny hole in the sleeve, and a bag of jacks with a red ball.

In the spring, Pompey showed her how to fish in the creek and allowed her to wade in the cool waters. She caught crickets and butterflies and watched *The Beverly Hillbillies* and *Dark Shadows* and *I Dream of Genie* and *Popeye* and *Underdog* and *Green Acres* on Pompey's fuzzy, black and white television. She washed dishes and swept the floor and washed out their clothes and pinned them on a clothesline. And when storm season came about, Pompey told her what to do if the storm was a hurricane.

Leatha made herself a close and best friend to Savonne. Leatha followed the girl everywhere, even into the creek waters where Savonne liked to wade her feet and watch the minnows. Savonne never had a dog before, and she didn't really care to have it around her that much.

One night on the front porch, Leatha came up to Savonne and put her front paws on the girl's knees and accidentally scratched her.

Savonne pushed the dog away and said, "I hate that dog. It follows me everywhere and barks at me and always wantin to jump on me and sleep next to me, so I can't stretch out my legs cause of her ole lumpy body bein in the way. And she won't move. I always have to push her away."

"Leatha? You hate Leatha? She tryin be your friend and you hate her?"

"She always following me, and she barks too much."

"Don't you know about dogs, girl?" Pompey said. "Dogs are the best thing that ever happened to people. Way back when God got mad at Adam and Eve and kicked them out of Eden, it was a dog that followed them out the garden gate and stayed with them and hunted food and slept with them at night to keep them warm when they didn't know how to make their own way. And dogs don't ask for nothin in return cept a little scratch behind the ears and some leftovers."

Pompey scratched his own ear, stuck a finger in, and pulled out some ear wax. He looked at it, rolled it between his fingers, and dusted it off against his overalls.

"Over everything else, dogs choose to be our best friends. Dogs live for us. If they didn't, they'd be wolves."

Pompey shook out a cigarette from a crumpled pack he had in the chest pocket of his overalls, put it between his lips, and went into the kitchen for a wooden match. He came out, struck the match on the door frame, lit the cigarette, took a drag, and blew out a spout of wispy white smoke.

He looked around. Savonne was still sitting back in the big rocking chair but not rocking. All he could see from where he stood under the porch light was ankles marked by mosquito bites and feet in faded red tennis shoes.

"I don't want to hear you say you hate Leatha no more, girl. And you better not push her off the bed when she sleep wit you at night, cause she there to protect your skinny butt. Member dat."

Pompey leaned against the side of the porch and looked out at the overgrown yard.

"Every dog is a good dog, girl. Every dog got a heart as pure as rainwater. Them dogs that fight and bite? They'd be good dogs too if it weren't for people teachin em to act crazy like that."

Pompey took another drag from his cigarette, savoring the feeling of the smoke raking down to his lungs.

"Even them feral dogs that walk around the junkyard sometimes. I bet you they'd give their back dew claws to have somebody take them in and feed them and let them sleep in a bed."

Pompey flicked ashes from the end of his cigarette. The ashes floated and lazily swirled away on the evening breeze.

"You better spect Leatha and pet her when you think about it cause she spects you. And check her for ticks every now and then, you hear me girl?"

Savonne nodded, wishing that Pompey would stop talking about dogs and going on about how great they was.

Pompey fell silent for a minute, pushing something around in his mind. Savonne wasn't watching his face, she was picking at her finger nails, waiting for the lightning bugs to start their flickering. Glad Pompey went silent for a minute.

"I'm thinkin I might give you Leatha since she like you so much."

Savonne didn't say anything.

"From now on, Leatha is your dog, girl. I'm givin her to you."

"Okay," Savonne said softly.

The first lightning bug flicked by and Savonne put her hand out. The lightning bug landed on her thumb, flashed its small beacon of light just once, and flew away.

A few more appeared, hovering above the grass in the yard, flashing their lights at each other. Savonne jumped out of the rocking chair and ran into the yard to play with the lightning bugs. Leatha followed her.

*

One day in early August of 1969, Pompey got it in his mind to shoot himself. His stomach had been hurting him for weeks and he knew it wasn't going away. He was spitting up blood some days and coughing up black bile on others.

He was old and tired and the only thing that was stopping him was his granddaughter Savonne. But the pain was getting to him. He couldn't hold to a life much longer with all that pain. Didn't know what to do with the girl though. She was eleven now and could walk herself to the grocery and let Sally know he was dead. Sally would call the police and they'd take Savonne to her granny in Indiana. He hadn't heard from Coco since she brought the girl to him. Police wouldn't know where to look for her neither. Sometimes, he worried about Coco. Even went up to Sally's and used her phone to call Neicey.

"You hear from Coco yet?"

"Not a word."

"Where'd she get off too?"

"Told me she tryin' California for a while."

"Did she say when she comin back?"

"No, she did not."

"Christ make me a god damned holy ghost!"

"You gettin tired of the girl? You want me come get her? If I do, I'm takin her straight to the police. Cause I ain't takin care a no daughter that Coco just dumped off like some goddamned stray puppy."

Pompey hung up on his daughter. She still mad about him leaving her mother all those years ago. Still mad cause he spent the last half of his life chasing the bottle and mad cause Coco didn't turn out the way Neicey wanted.

He drank a half swig of vodka and thought his stomach was put on fire. He went to the outhouse and wretched out blood and vodka. He'd gotten drunk the night before, and his stomach was still burning from the vodka he drank yesterday. He knew this wasn't no curse or conjure. This was what came from old age and drinking. When it was over, he went to Savonne and said, "Where my handgun?"

Savonne said, "I don't know."

"It was right here yesterday on the mantel in the metal box. Ain't here now and only you and me and Leatha been in here since the last time I saw it. And I know for sure it weren't Leatha, and sure as the Devil burns balls it weren't me who took it."

"You was drunked up yesterday. You was shootin up the cars. Maybe you took it and put it somewhere else."

"Where you hide it?"

"I didn't hide it, Pompey, I didn't touch it," Savonne said.

"Where you hide my gun?" he yelled.

Pompey waited for her to answer, but she just shook her head. He couldn't stay being mad at her. She was so skinny and slight. Her lower lip was trembling. She had a hurt look deep in her eyes. Pompey felt a pang of remorse for letting his temper up. And what she said could be true. He could have left the gun somewhere else.

Pompey went into the bedroom, looked everywhere for it but couldn't find it. He went to the kitchen then looked around the porch and couldn't find it there either. Pompey spied something shining like metal in the sun. Sitting on the concrete, next to the hand pump, was the handgun that he called Pistol Pete. Pompey went into his bedroom with the gun and locked the door behind.

From behind the shut door, Pompey yelled, "Savonne, somethin happen to me, you go on down to Sally's and tell her to call the police."

"What?"

"You heard me."

Savonne was quiet for a moment, thinking.

"Diamond John comin to get you?" Savonne ventured.

"No, no."

"Gator?"

"I ain't seen a gator round here in twenty years. I told you that. Snakes is what you gotta be wary of."

"I know. Copperheads."

"Yes, girl. Copperheads. Rattlers. Cottonmouths."

"What's gonna happen to you?"

Savonne didn't think it was fair to say something might happen to him but not tell what it is.

"Nothin gonna happen to me. I'm just tellin you what to do if somethin does happen."

"Hurricane comin?"

"No, not a hurricane comin."

"What then?"

"Go down to the creek and get us some minnows to fish with tomorrow."

"What gonna happen, Pompey?"

"Jesus the hell goddam it, just do what I say."

Savonne took the red coffee can and ran to the creek and away from Pompey. Leatha went with her.

Pompey waited until he heard the screen door slam, then he laid down on his bed. "Papa Legba," he said, "Open the gates. Need to ask for some help for Savonne."

*

When Savonne came back, that afternoon, Pompey still hadn't come out of his room with his hands shaking and dried spittle streaked across the side of his face, like he always did after he slept off a drunk. Savonne knew something was wrong. Pompey said something might happen. Wouldn't tell her just what though.

She went to the door and listened. She heard nothing.

"Pompey?"

No answer. She knocked on the door. Still nothing. She tried the doorknob. Locked. She went into the kitchen and sat at the table, thinking, wondering what was going on. A terrible thought came to mind. What if Pompey wasn't in there? What if he decided to go back to Natchez like he threatened to do whenever he got sad about being old or when he got mad at her cause she was playing in the rusted cars? What if he just lit off and didn't bother to tell her?

She went outside, closed the front door behind her and went around to Pompey's window. The window shade was down, but she could see a few flies on the pane. She tapped on the pane. No answer. She tapped harder. Nothing. She wondered if Diamond John had been there. She never saw Diamond John before, but Pompey told her stories about him. How mean he was and how bad he wanted Pompey's conjure book, and what fearful things he would do with it. Diamond John could've took Pompey's life or made him take his own and left with the conjure book before she got back from the creek.

"Pompeee," she yelled at the top of her lungs.

Again, just quiet. She went to Pompey's tool shed, took a hammer, ran back with it, and hit the windowpane. It broke in a round pattern and crackled apart. Warm air that smelled of shit flew through the window. She hammered at the remaining shards of glass. If Pompey was not sick or dying, she knew by now he would be awake and bellowing cuss words at her for breaking through the window. She heard nothing but the sound of flies buzzing and the far-off sound of a car passing on the gravel road. It took a few minutes to pull herself up through the window. She was a tall girl for her age but still the window was too high for her to get through easily. She fell into Pompey's bedroom.

He was there, lying in bed. He had a pillow over his face. The pillow had a burnt hole in the middle of it and feathers lying around it. Savonne took one hand and slowly lifted the pillow.

Pompey's face was slack and his mouth was half open, eyes closed, tiny round black hole in the middle of his head. Much of the sheet and the pillowcase was soaked in dark blood, spread out underneath his head. She covered her mouth, but bile surged up from her stomach. She ran past Pompey's body, afraid he was going to flash out a dead arm and pull her into the netherworld with him

She unlocked the door and ran into the living room. Then through the front door and to the well. She took the hand pump and pumped until water splashed up into the metal bucket. She pumped until the bucket was half full. Savonne took it and poured the water over her hair and face. Pompey was dead and she was all alone. Savonne wondered if Diamond John knew Pompey was dead or if he killed Pompey with a conjure and was on his way there to get the conjure book.

She went away from the house. Leatha saw her and jumped up from her resting place to follow her down the path to the gravel road and on to Sally's grocery. Savonne opened the door and the bell jingled. Only Sally was there, sitting at the counter fanning herself from the heavy morning heat.

"You come for Pompey's check? I got it here. I can cash it for you if you want to buy something," Sally said.

Savonne almost blurted it out. Pompey was dead. Pompey was laid up in his stinky bed with flies doing the two-step over his face.

Instead, Savonne just nodded. She felt tears burning behind her eyes and she knew she was gonna start crying.

"What's wrong?" Sally said loudly. "Why you hair all wet?"

Savonne cleared her throat, shook her head, trying not to show her emotions. No. Savonne decided not to tell just yet.

"Pompey whupped me, told me to come down here and fetch the money from his check and a pound of rice."

"What Pompey whip you for?"

"I was... I was playing in the cars again. And Pompey..."

Savonne started crying. Sally came from behind the counter.

"Girly-girl, don't you cry now. Pompey just get worried. Snakes live up in those old heaps and you could git bit."

Savonne nodded.

"I know, I know."

Savonne wiped at her eyes and her nose.

"Pompey be needin a bag of rice, he tole me. And two Reese's Cups."

Sally smiled down at Savonne.

"You gonna be alright?"

Savonne nodded.

Sally went to the store shelf, brought down the rice Savonne ordered, went into the big freezer, brought out two chilled Reese's Cups, put it all in an oversized brown paper bag, and went to the cash register.

36

She opened the envelope, pulled out Pompey's check, read it out loud, "Seventy dollars," and subtracted fifty-four cents.

Sally counted out the money to Savonne and placed each bill in her small, thin hand. When Sally got to the last dollar bill she pulled it back.

"Fee for cashing the check," Sally said and stuffed the dollar bill into her bra, smoothed out her blouse, and handed Savonne the coin change and the sack of groceries.

Savonne walked home and put the brown paper bag on the porch floor. Leatha came behind her and walked up to the porch and sat next to the rocking chair. Savonne tucked the money from the check in her overalls pocket. She couldn't go in the house again. Not with Pompey's dead body in there. She went to the front door, scared. She heard nothing. She put her ear to the door. No sound, but she didn't open the door.

She went off the porch and around the house, walking wide away from it and headed toward the dead cars, moving down the dried mud rows, looking left and right for one that she could get in and lay down in and let the heat bake into her body. She found an old truck with a loose door and got into the cab. She laid her body down. She was all alone. Again. She felt the cross around her neck. She touched the money in her pocket. She thought about Pompey and how he looked, laying there dead. She began to cry silently because she was scared and sad.

Time drifted around her and she stayed still, unmoving, unbending, warm tears running from her eyes down the side of her face and into her ears and hair. She cried quietly for a long time and when sleep came upon her, she fought it until her eyes hurt and her brain went dizzy. She fought it until the sky became dusky and the moon got lost behind a herd of blue clouds. She fell asleep as the night turned to pitch and the air blew cool into the window and around her.

Savonne woke up when she felt something moving, sliding over her leg, something dry and rough like linen paper. She saw the head of a tiny brown snake inching toward her and she knew in her heart that Diamond John had sent it.

The snake snapped its head down and bit her on the kneecap. She kicked and thrashed until the snake let go and moved away from her. She could see it had another head. It had two heads, identical, eyes shiny as glass, looking straight into her face, one head turned to her, then the other. She knew for sure, if it struck again, it would kill her. She grabbed it by its tail and flung it out the window of the truck. She looked down at her knee where the one head had bit her. Two small dots of blood welled up from under her skin. In the moonlight, she could see it didn't get in real deep. Even so, her skin swelled up around the bite. She opened the door of the truck and saw Leatha running toward her. She stumbled down, looking for the snake to come slithering toward her. No snake.

Leatha guided her silently toward the house. Savonne didn't make it. She fell beside the house and stayed there on the dried mud. She felt Leatha's face next to hers, smelled Leatha's nasty dog breath, as she passed back into the land of dreams.

In some places, it is said that if someone passes over and lives to tell about it, that person will carry strong magic into the conscious world. Savonne passed over.

It was bright there, sunny and warm. Her daddy was there, and she knew for sure he was no longer part of the conscious world. Her daddy bent down, wrapped her up in a hug, and kissed her forehead. They were in a field of grass that smelled fresh and slightly lemony. Then her daddy said, "A Mojo man is coming, but you will be strong. Use the book."

"The Bible, Daddy?" Savonne asked.

"No," her daddy shook his head. "He knows ways around The Bible. Another book. Of the old religion."

Her daddy touched Savonne's cheek and smoothed his palm over Savonne's crazy hair. He smiled down at her.

"You go on back, now."

*

It was hot. A warm breeze ruffled Savonne's hair. It was an hour after noon and the sun was shining through a thin blue sky. Savonne opened her eyes. Leatha was still there, her body draped over Savonne's stomach, her head lying limp, nose touching the hard earth.

Savonne lifted up on her elbows and felt a heavy, sharp pain between her eyes and behind her ears. Her leg felt hot and pain shot up from her knee. She was dizzy. She touched her fingers to where the snake had struck. The skin around the two tiny punctures felt crusty under her fingertips.

Savonne nudged Leatha to get her off her stomach. Leatha did not move. Savonne didn't realize that Leatha had stayed with her throughout the night, licking off the pinpoints of blood and snake venom, protecting her from the snake when it came to bite again.

Savonne didn't know that Leatha had been savagely bit and was almost dead from the poison of the two-headed snake, and that Leatha caught the snake under her paw, bit through its body, killed it, and carried the dead snake's body in her mouth to the high grass at the edge of the automobile graveyard. Leatha stayed with Savonne through the worrisome night and only when Leatha sensed that Savonne was alive and awake did she let her weakened old canine heart shut down. Savonne didn't understand what a miracle it was that she survived the night.

Savonne gently tried to shake Leatha awake, then picked her body up off her stomach and, limping from the snakebite, carried Leatha down to the creek. Savonne laid Leatha's body at the side of the creek. Savonne stroked her hand over the dog's head and neck.

"Wake up, Leatha," Savonne pleaded. "Please wake up."

Savonne watched for any small sign of movement or breathing or tail wagging. When none came, she felt her heart break and her eyes burn with tears.

Savonne went into the creek waters, dipped some into her cupped hands and brought it back. She held it to Leatha's snout.

"Here's some water. It'll make you feel better."

Leatha did not move. A couple of gnats lit on her face and proceeded to crawl around the inside edges of her eyes.

"I'm sorry, Leatha, I never did really hate you. I never did. I love you. Please wake up. Please?"

Savonne sprinkled water over Leatha's forehead hoping the wetness would revive her. When the water didn't work, Savonne took Leatha's face in her hands and looked closely at the dog.

"Please don't be dead, please," Savonne whispered.

Savonne realized Leatha was growing cold. The fur on her forehead began to feel different and was shedding a little out on Savonne's hand. Savonne picked up Leatha's front paws and let them go. They fell back, limp and lifeless.

*

Savonne had to go back into the house but she didn't want to cause Pompey's dead body was still in there. What if he came alive, animated by the invisible hand of Diamond John, and he tried to kill her? What if the snake had crawled into the house? What if she didn't go back in and just ran on down the road?

She had to find the conjure book, and she wanted to get a blanket to cover up Leatha. And she needed her clothes. And her toothbrush and her old change purse with three dollars in quarters, nickels and dimes. She felt in her pocket. The money from Pompey's check was still tucked in. Money enough to travel back to Indianapolis. But the conjure book was in the house somewhere. She had to go in.

The most likely place to look for the conjure book would be in Pompey's bedroom, where his dead body was, but she couldn't make herself do it. She had a hard time pushing down the fear she felt in her brain and in her heart when she entered the house to fetch the other things she needed. The fear of going into his bedroom was even worse. She quickly kicked off her flip flops and put on her tennis shoes.

Savonne yelled at the top of her lungs: "Pompey, are you really dead?"

No answer.

"If you ain't dead, tell me now."

No answer.

"Pompey, if you dead and you a ghost wantin to do me some harm, tell me now so I can run right out this house."

No answer.

"Pompey, where's the book?"

No answer. Just quiet and the ticking of the wall clock in the kitchen.

"Where's the conjure book," she whispered, and out of the corner of her eye she saw something fly by her face. She turned around. It was a lightning bug, drowsily flitting through the heavy warm air of the house. Savonne stood perfectly still and followed the lightning bug with her eyes. It went on into the kitchen and through to the living room. It landed on the threadbare recliner that Pompey liked to use for his afternoon naps. Savonne walked softly into the living room and over to the recliner, watching the lightning bug, understanding that it might have been sent by Pompey.

She got on her knees and felt her hand under the recliner. Nothing. She lifted the seat cushion and pushed her hand down in the spaces between the arms and the seat. Nothing. She pushed her skinny arm in deeper, and her fingers touched paper. She slid her fingers around it and pulled out a tiny leather-bound book with loose paper pages, tied with a thin red ribbon.

She knew this had to be the conjure book or what was left of it. She went to her cot and took the blanket off. She needed to cover up Leatha. She didn't want the dog's body to be covered with flies and maggots, but she didn't have time to bury her. With the conjure book safe and tucked under her arm, and the blanket in her hands, she ran out of the house and down to Leatha.

Savonne put the blanket over her dog. She dropped to her knees, bowed her head, prayed to God to call up Leatha's soul to heaven, and prayed to her daddy to guide her and help her find the way to Indianapolis. She walked from the creek, blinking back tears. Leatha had been her best friend. Now Leatha was gone too.

Heavy clouds clumped over the sky like dirty cotton balls. New Orleans was seventeen miles away. Savonne knew that because Pompey told her that if she was bad and didn't do her chores, he would make her walk all seventeen miles to New Orleans and go live with Niecey and evil old Diamond John.

Savonne knew she could walk the seventeen miles and go to the Greyhound Station to catch a bus back to Indianapolis, but it was now mid-afternoon, and it might be dark before she got there.

She went around the side of the house and caught her breath. A black pick-up truck was parked in the yard, directly in front of the porch. The inside of the truck was empty. Had to be Diamond John. He had to know that Pompey had passed over, and now he was there for the precious conjure book.

Savonne retreated to the creek as quickly and quietly as she could, ran past Leatha's body, crossed the shallow waters, and ran into a field of weeds. She crouched down and watched the house from the cover of wildflowers and blackberry brambles. The bugs and bees found her and buzzed around her head like tiny airplanes. She hoped no snakes would come slithering toward her.

A moment later, Diamond John emerged from the front door he had broken, holding Pompey's shotgun. He put his hand up to his broad forehead and looked around. He spied the brown paper bag, grabbed it up with one hand, and emptied the contents on the floor of the porch. He kicked the melted Reese's cups off the porch, and took the bag of rice to his truck and threw it in. He left the empty paper bag on the porch and walked around toward the automobile graveyard. He walked fast, carrying the shotgun, crunching the dried mud trails, moving like a wolf between the dead cars and abandoned trucks.

"Little girl," he called. "Come on out."

He stopped at the truck that Savonne had slept in the night before. The driver's side door was still open. Diamond John put his hand on the seat and swiped at something on the seat upholstery.

"Blood," Savonne whispered to herself. "My blood."

Diamond John looked at his fingers, sniffed at them with his big nostrils, and wiped the blood on the side of his pants. He smiled a broad smile, and the diamond in his tooth caught on the sunlight and flashed like lightning.

"Little girl," he called again. He walked on past the truck.

"You dead yet, little girl? Copperhead poison got you yet?"

Pompey always told Savonne if anything happened to his daughter, Neicey, Diamond John would be coming after the conjure book. Savonne thought maybe Neicey was dead too or maybe she just up and left. Maybe Neicey fell out of love with this scary-eyed, Voodoo-loving giant of a man, so she divorced him.

If Neicey left him, Savonne reasoned, and Pompey was dead, nothing could keep Diamond John from taking the conjure book. Specially not a skinny little girl still weak from a snake bite. Savonne touched her knee, felt the tender skin around the crusted puncture wounds. Diamond John sent the two-headed snake to kill her. Made her think maybe Diamond John conjured Pompey to shoot himself in the forehead. Or Diamond John did it himself.

Savonne scooted into the thicker part of the weeds, and stifled a wince from the pain of getting prickled by blackberry thorns.

Diamond John kept walking around the dead vehicles. Looking under some of them, looking behind him at the house every now and then. After a long time of searching, he started back to the house.

"I didn't kill him," Diamond John shouted. "But I knew he was dead. I could make you dead too. But I won't. Not if you show yourself."

He kept walking, his head cocked to hear any sounds of Savonne.

"You don't even have to show yourself. Just yell out where I can find the conjure book and I'll let you live."

Diamond John held up Pompey's shotgun, unloaded it, and held up the shotgun shells.

"See? The gun ain't loaded. I won't shoot you."

All he got was silence from Savonne.

He made a show of putting the shells in his pocket. He went to the front of the house, walked up the porch, and through the front door.

She heard things inside the house being moved around. Books being thrown. The squeal of table legs moving over the wooden floor. Cabinet doors being slammed. Diamond John was searching hard for the conjure book. After a few minutes he stomped out the front door. He stopped on the porch.

"Tell me where it is," he yelled.

Savonne didn't move. She was so scared she dropped the conjure book. It landed softly in the briars in front of her feet. She willed herself to not make a sound.

Finally, Diamond John got into his big black truck. He turned on the engine and pulled out.

"I know you out there, little girl," he yelled. "Nobody gonna protect you now."

Savonne stayed in her hiding place for a long time after he left, scared to move, thinking she'd be seen if he suddenly came back. Finally, she picked up the conjure book and ran to the house.

She grabbed the paper bag, put in the conjure book, then hesitantly went back into the house. She gathered up some clothes, her toothbrush, her hairbrush, and the old change purse full of coins.

She ran with her paper bag, slammed the broken door, ran down the dirt road, and didn't stop until she got to the gravel road. She stood for a moment in the gravel, looking for a big black truck. Instead, a sky-blue convertible Cadillac went by, driven by a white man wearing overalls and sunglasses with a head full of wispy, white hair. He didn't even turn to look at her. She saw the license plate as the long car rolled on, saw that it was from the state of Indiana. Savonne wondered if somebody was giving her a sign. She waited until the Caddy was out of sight and began walking in the same direction.

Savonne walked the dusty gravel road, holding the

brown paper bag in front of her, ready to run if she spied a black truck. She walked past Sally's grocery and saw Sally through the window. She was sitting behind the cash register, reading a True Romance. Savonne walked past Dumont's farm where that crazy speckled horse named Bucephalus galloped up to the fence and walked beside her, prancing and naying and shaking its head like it wanted to tell her something. She yelled "Go away" at the horse, and it whinnied and snorted at her in some ancient horse language and kept doing it until she got past the fence. Bucephalus stood on his back legs and punched his front hoofs through the air. Savonne looked for a moment and saw the wild look in the horse's eyes. She turned around and walked steadily on as the sounds of the stomping and naying got fainter and fainter, until she couldn't hear it any longer. She turned around again and saw Bucephalus with his head in the grass, peacefully cutting off mouthfuls with his big flat teeth, and chewing.

Finally, the road changed to blacktop and about a half mile further down, Savonne came to a four-way crossroads. She'd never been this far down this road before. She didn't know which way went to New Orleans, so she stood there trying to figure it out, a little panicked that Diamond John might drive up and snatch her life away. The sky was getting darker. The clouds were bumping together, and she heard a soft rumble of thunder. She feared she'd be walking in the rain. A few moments later, a green sedan pulled up to the crossroads and stopped, engine idling, car humming and rumbling. A white man smoking a cigar was behind the wheel. He wore an old-fashioned fedora cocked to one side. A tan-skinned woman wearing sunglasses, ruby red lipstick, a stylish pageboy haircut, and a pearl necklace, sat beside him. The woman looked at Savonne and smiled brightly.

Savonne smiled back but held her bag of possessions closer to her chest.

"Little girl," the woman said. "Do you want us to take you home? We can drive you."

Savonne noticed the woman had a tiny pale heart tattooed on her upper cheek which was partially hidden by her sunglasses.

The man took the cigar out of his mouth and said, "Where you headin with that paper bag full of clothes?"

"To my granny's house."

"Where that be?

"Indianapolis."

"Indianapolis? That's mighty far."

"How you plan on gettin there?" the woman asked.

Savonne shook her head. Looked down at her feet.

"I don't know. Greyhound bus, I magine."

"We'll take you," the woman said. "We'll take you to Indianapolis. We was lookin for you."

"Lookin for me? Why? Do you know me?"

"Pompey sent us," the man said.

The woman turned her face away and coughed.

"Davie. That cigar."

"Pompey?"

"No, he's just kidding you," the woman said. "We just want you to come away from here, and we'll get you to Indianapolis."

"I'll just keep walkin," Savonne said and started walking fast.

The sedan jerked forward and moved at the same speed.

The woman said, "Honey, you at a crossroads. You right to walk away as fast as you can."

The man said, "The Louisiana Devil hangs round here."

"How you know?"

"Just do," the woman answered.

"Papa Legba, what some people call him," the man said.

"No, Davie. Legba no devil. He just minds the crossroads, tricks people a little, might open the gates and let them talk to the spirits, if he likes them. But there's a devil round here alright, Honey. That horse you passed down the road? He was tryin to tell you."

"You a colored, aren't you, girl?"

The man flicked ashes out the car window. The woman slapped the man lightly on his arm.

"Of course she colored, Davie. My lordy, what kind of question is that?"

Savonne nodded her head.

"Then you should know all about that Papa Legba," Davie said.

"All I know is I want to get home and see my granny. Gwen is her first name. People call her Mama Gwen."

"What if your granny moved away? And she not waiting to find you anymore? What you gonna do?" Davie asked.

Savonne stopped walking.

"Why you say that?"

"Oh he's just tryin to scare you. Stop tryin to scare her, Davie. He don't know your granny. He never even been up to Indianapolis. But I have. I went last year, 1966."

"That was not last year," Davie said.

"That wasn't last year? Oh my goodness. I got it wrong? And time is supposed to be my forte."

"Yeah but you never could figure out clocks."

"Anyways, they all crashed that year. Well, eleven of them did. It was so exciting. Just chaos. Saw all the race cars and the race car drivers."

The woman suddenly stuck out her tongue and rolled it back in. Savonne was startled by the action.

"Wherever you go, you causin chaos, woman," Davie said.

"Just my nature."

"My granny still waitin for me to get home," Savonne said.

"Oh my. Davie!"

The woman pointed toward the other side of the road.

"There's a snake crawling across the road."

Savonne could see a brown and tan snake coming out if the weeds, slipping and curling its way across the blacktop. She recognized it. Copperhead. And big as a viper.

"Get in the car girl," Davie said.

"Shoot, could be that Louisiana Devil come for you," the woman said.

"Get in," Davie commanded.

The woman let out a sharp laugh.

The man put the gear in park, got out of the car, quickly opened the back door and said, "Get in the car, girl, before that snake gets you."

Savonne looked at the snake still making its way across the road. She looked at the woman who was now intently watching the snake. She looked at the snake again and it changed direction, veering toward her now instead of straight across the road. Savonne scrambled into the car.

The man closed the door, went to the driver's seat, jumped in, and took off, squealing tires. He aimed the car to the right, ran over the snake, braked, pulled the gear in reverse, and backed the car over the snake, braked again, pulled the gear into drive, went forward, and ran over it yet again. He pushed down hard on the gas, and they sped away. Savonne looked out the rear window, the snake had stopped moving and was flattened out in a few places. She knew it was dead.

"Ain't that funny," the woman said. "We were just talking about the Devil and here come a big ole snake cross the road. Gives me the shivers."

"We going to New Orleans," Davie said. "We can take you to the Greyhound station. But first I got to stop and get gas."

Ten minutes later, Davie pulled into a Shell station. A man in coveralls came out and pumped two dollars' worth of premium ethyl into the sedan. Davie walked to a pay phone that was situated in the front of the gas station.

"Can I call my granny?" Savonne asked the woman as she watched Davie deposit coin after coin.

"You can call her at the Greyhound station. Now when Davie gets back to the car, I'm going over to that soda pop machine and buy me a cold bottle of Coke. You want one?"

"Yes," Savonne answered. A few minutes later, Davie hung up the pay phone and walked to the car. He paid the gas attendant and got back in the driver's seat.

"We got another job," he said to the woman.

"Another one? Where at?"

"At the Tuscaloosa place."

"When?"

"Soon. Tonight."

"Oh my Davie. We still haven't finished this one."

"Don't think you'll want to say no. Pays too good. And it'll give you the chance to do what you love to do the most."

"What's that?" the woman said.

Davie smiled. "Make chaos."

The woman looked at Savonne.

"Let's get to New Orleans first. Finish the trip. Then you can tell me what you talkin about."

Davie nodded.

"Right now, I'm going to get Vonny some Cokes. You want one too?"

"Sure."

"Why you callin me Vonny?"

"That's your name isn't it?" the woman said.

"Only my mama call me that," Savonne said.

"Pompey said never to call her Vonny, remember?" Davie said.

"I thought he said to call her Vonny?"

"No, he says that's what her mama calls her and not to call her that," Davie answered.

"How you talk to Pompey? I thought Pompey was dead," Savonne said.

"I'm sorry. He is dead, Vonny," the woman answered.

"My name is Savonne."

"It's not Vonny?"

"I never told my name to you."

"Oh."

It was early evening and softly raining when the sedan pulled up next to the Greyhound station. Buses were leaving one after another after another. The faces in the bus windows flashed by like actors in a black-and-white movie. Savonne watched from the backseat of the car. Davie parked right outside the big bright front door. She was a little bit nervous about the whole thing.

Savonne didn't know much about the Greyhound bus, never been on one. She saw commercials on Pompey's television, and everybody looked happy. It looked like the easiest thing to do: ride the Greyhound, leave the driving to them.

"Sure you don't want us to take you all the way?"

"No. I can do it on my own."

"You got enough money for your ticket?" the woman asked.

"Yes."

"You got enough coins to call your granny long distance and tell her you on the way home?"

"Yes."

"Hurry up and get on one of those buses, now. Diamond John might be closing in," Davie said.

"You know Diamond John?"

"Yes. No. I'm just jokin. I just made that name up. I don't know nothin about no Diamond John or Jack Ruby, or Pearl Buck, or nobody named after precious stones."

"Why you say Diamond John might be closin in?"

The woman lightly slapped the man on the arm.

"Now see, you done alarmed the child. Talking about things you don't know about," the woman said.

"Get on out of the car now, we goin to another somebody that needs our help."

"What you say about Diamond John?" Savonne asked.

"Don't forget your paper bag, girl," Davie said.

"Get out the car now," the woman said softly.

Savonne grabbed the paper bag, opened the car door, and slid out. She turned to close the door and the woman said, "Have a good trip home."

Davie started the engine, and left Savonne on the sidewalk, in the rain, in front of the lit-up Greyhound station. Savonne went into the bus station and stopped at the first kindly looking person she saw.

"I need to get on the bus to Indianapolis," Savonne said to a woman that was sitting in a plastic seat with a brown suitcase on the seat next to her.

"You have to buy a ticket. Go over there to the ticket window. They'll help you."

Savonne went to the window and a man with thick glasses and a mustache asked could he help her.

"Yes," Savonne said. "I want a ticket to Indianapolis."

"No tickets straight to Indianapolis," the man with the mustache said. "Have to go to Memphis, then to Indianapolis. You buy two tickets. One to Memphis $15.99 and $13.55, the total is $29.54. And you better hurry, the bus to Memphis is leaving in…eight minutes."

Savonne dug down into her pocket and came up with a twenty and a ten-dollar bill.

She handed the money to the man. He handed her two tickets and some change.

"Where do I get on at?"

"Terminal three."

Savonne looked around.

"To your left," he said and pointed.

Savonne grabbed her paper bag and walked toward the terminal. She had less than eight minutes, and she wanted to call her grandmother.

She remembered the phone number from when she was little. She put in a dime and called the number. A woman's voice came on and said she first had to dial the area code.

Savonne didn't know the area code. But she asked what the code was for Indianapolis. The lady's voice told her and said she needed to put in thirty-five cents more. Savonne went into her pocket, brought out the change, and put it into coin slot.

"What number please?"

Savonne told her the number.

Granny answered in her high, loud voice.

"Hello?"

Savonne said, "Granny? This is Savonne?"

Savonne heard the phone receiver drop, clattering. Then Granny picked it up.

"Savonne?" She was almost shouting.

"Yes?"

"Is that really you?"

"It's me."

"Savonne? Oh my God, Savonne?"

"Yes, Granny?"

"Are you all right? Where you at? I'll come get you. Savonne? Oh my God. Savonne?"

"I'm all right. Got to catch my bus though. I'm goin to Memphis first, then Indianapolis."

"I'll come get you. Tell me where you at. Are you all right?"

Her granny's voice got scratchy with tears.

"I'll leave right now, just tell me where you at."

"I'm at the Greyhound station, Granny. In New Orleans. I already bought my tickets. I gotta go. My bus is leavin. I love you, Granny.”

She hung up and walked quickly toward terminal three, she had six minutes.

“Vonny,” she heard someone call. The voice was familiar. Sounded like that strange woman in the green car, but she didn’t turn around. She was in a hurry.

Savonne kept walking, got to the terminal, got to the bus, handed her ticket to the bus driver, and boarded the bus. She walked to the back and took a seat at the very last row. She watched as other passengers got on.

The bus was almost full when she saw them: the two who picked her up at the crossroads. The tan-skinned woman—but now she was lighter skinned, looking like a white woman—with her boyfriend named Davie. Savonne saw the woman enter the bus. Davie stepped behind the woman and was standing at the bottom step of the bus, blocking the entrance to the bus. The woman talked low and quick to the bus driver. The bus driver nodded once and looked back at Savonne.

“Vonny,” the woman suddenly said, loudly. “We was worried sick about you. Runnin away again.”

The woman walked toward Savonne, Davie followed.

“Now come on with us and don’t give us no trouble, or we will call the police,” the woman said.

“Third time the girl run away,” Davie exclaimed to nobody in particular.

“Such a wild child,” the woman said. “Now come on with us, don’t cause a delay here on this Greyhound bus. These people need to get goin.”

The woman looked at the bus driver.

“Her Auntie used to cook and clean for us. Now this girl got her so worried and upset, she had to go in the hospital."

Savonne said, "That ain't true, and I told you I ain't goin with you. I'm goin home."

"Let's go call the police honey," the woman said. "They make her go with us."

"See what you make us do, Vonny," the man named Davie said.

"My name ain't Vonny, my name is Savonne."

Davie grabbed Savonne's arm in an iron grip.

"Don't fight us," he whispered. "Pompey don't want us to let you go. He tole us to take you the whole way. Afraid the snakes'll get you."

Savonne didn't budge. She held on to her seat as long as she could, until it took both of them to pry her out.

The man grabbed Savonne's brown paper bag and the woman walked behind Savonne, pushing Savonne's shoulders forward until they were off the bus.

"You're causing us so much trouble."

Savonne heard a scream, and another scream, coming from the bus from which she was just forcibly taken. People were running out of the bus.

Savonne heard the bus driver yell "Snake!"

"See?" the woman said. "He sent a snake for you. Put it on the damn bus."

"Voodoo Hoodoo," Davie said.

"We gonna have to drive her, Davie. Like Pompey wanted."

"Long way to Indianapolis."

"We driving her. That's what we were asked to do."

"Got to stop in Tuscaloosa first."

*

Davie opened the door of the sedan for Savonne. She didn't want to go. These people weren't right. Maybe they were as bad as Diamond John. Maybe they want the conjure book too. Why they keep talking about Pompey?

"Why you doin this?" Savonne asked as she climbed into the back seat.

"We told you, Vonny, Pompey sent us," the woman said.

"My name is Savonne."

"Oh."

"How you know Pompey?"

"We don't know him. He asked a friend of ours, who asked us to come help you out."

"I saw Pompey, he looked dead."

"He is dead," Davie answered.

Savonne grew quiet and stayed like that for a long time thinking about Pompey. How could he be dead but telling people to come and help her?

"What your name?" Savonne finally said to the woman.

"Honey, you couldn't pronounce my name even if I told you twice."

"Let me try."

The woman turned to Savonne and said, "Okay my name is——."

Savonne saw the woman's mouth move but, she couldn't hear when she said the word for her name. Savonne saw the woman's skin was back to brown. The color of oak wood.

"What is it?" Savonne said. "Say it again?"

"Not saying it again."

Davie said, "People call her Kali. Just call her that, call her Kali."

"Yes Vonny. Call me Kali."

"My name is Savonne."

"Oh."

"Why your skin keep changin?"

Kali didn't answer.

Davie laughed and laughed until Kali stuck out her tongue at him and he stopped.

*

By the time they got to Tuscaloosa, it was dark, but Savonne saw the sign announcing the name of the town and its population of 79,000.

They drove past the town and onto a two-lane blacktop that went to a thin road that ran through a bunch of trees. The sedan pulled up to a gravel driveway in front of a faded out, gray slat mansion. Davie turned off the car engine. Kali smiled at Savonne.

"Okay, Honey," Kali said. "We're staying here overnight. Tomorrow we start out to Indianapolis."

"Why can't we go tonight?"

Davie said, "Got to do some work first. Make some money. Get something to eat."

"Aren't you hungry, Sweetie?" Kali asked.

"Yes."

"There should be some fried chicken in there. And some mashed potatoes."

Davie got out and opened the car door for Savonne.

"I'll wait in the car," Savonne said.

"No you ain't," Davie said. "Snakes get you out here."

"I'll be okay."

"Get out, Honey," Kali said.

"Not goin in that scary house."

Davie took Savonne's arm and pulled her out of the car. Savonne grabbed her brown paper bag as she slid across the seat. Davie stood her up on the gravel.

"You a stubborn one ain't ya."

Savonne clutched her brown paper bag holding the conjure book and her clothes. Kali got out of the car and walked up the brick steps to a wide wraparound porch. She unlocked the door. Savonne saw her disappear into the house and a moment later, the lights inside the foyer came on.

Davie shut the car door and pulled Savonne up the steps and into the house.

As she sat in the kitchen at a Formica-topped table with a paper plate full of food, Savonne had to say to herself that the fried chicken was really good. So was the mashed potatoes and the rolls and the gravy.

She ate two pieces, dipped the drumstick into the potatoes and gravy, and sopped up the leftover gravy with a white bread roll. The chicken came out of a cardboard bucket. Savonne decided it was the best fried chicken she ever had, except for Pompey's.

After she finished, Savonne burped.

Davie ate a couple of pieces too, wiped his mouth, and said, "Put the lid over the leftover pieces. We can have the rest for breakfast tomorrow."

"How comes you ain't eatin?" Savonne said to Kali.

"Time for bed, honey," Kali answered. She went into another room and came out holding a pillow and a blanket.

Kali let Savonne brush her teeth and wash her face and hands at the kitchen sink. Savonne dried her hands on some napkins that smelled like fried chicken and grabbed her brown paper bag. Kali led her down the dimly lit hallway to a tiny bedroom painted bright pink. She went to a lamp that sat on a table beside a bed made of wrought iron and switched it on. The bed looked uncomfortable and old. It held a thin, lumpy mattress with a faded pink sheet cover. Kali crouched down and looked under the bed.

"I know you must be tired."

Kali laid the pillow and blanket on the bed and went to the window, checked the lock, and closed the dusty curtains. She went to the closet and looked in. She picked something off the closet shelf.

"Nothing in here but this old Cinderella coloring book," Kali said, waving it back and forth.

"You want it?"

Savonne shook her head. Kali threw the book back into the closet and closed the door.

"No snakes gonna get in here," she said. "You'll be safe enough."

"Okay. And we goin to Indianapolis tomorrow, that right?"

Kali smiled and Savonne noticed her skin color was different. Dark, almost pure black now, with a tinge of blue. The white heart was shining bright as a tiny flashlight.

"Yes, Vonny, first thing in the morning."

Kali walked out the bedroom, closing the door behind her.

"My name is not Vonny," Savonne whispered.

As Kali walked down the hallway, Savonne heard her say, "Oh."

*

Savonne took her shoes off and climbed into the lumpy bed. She turned off the lamp and tried to go to sleep but, it wasn't happening. She wasn't tired enough. Not yet. She put her hand over the cross around her neck and prayed to God to let her get back to her Granny. She clicked the lamp on, got out of the bed, took the conjure book out of the paper bag, and untied the red ribbon.

The first page was filled with symbols and faded words. In the middle of the page, in flowery script, was written:

Protection Spell
Ten Cowry shells
Blood Root
Hide of a deer
Three strands of hair from a white horse
The rib bone of a black cat
Say these words three times -
Pwoteje sa a timnoun nan vodou

Savonne said the words by sounding them out. She struggled for a minute, whispering what she thought was the correct way to say the strange words. She closed the book and tied the ribbon around it. She didn't know if she said the words right, and she didn't know where to get Cowry shells, and she had no idea how to get a piece of deer skin or the rib bone of a black cat. Doing the conjures from the book was going to be harder than she thought.

She put the book back into her paper bag and covered it with clothes and the little coin purse. Savonne turned off the lamp and closed her eyes.

Around midnight, Savonne woke up. She had been dreaming about a door. Someone was knocking on it from the other side and, she didn't want to open it. She was glad to be awake, but something was tapping at her window. She put on the lamp. The tapping was sporadic and uneven.

"Who's there?" Savonne said.

No answer but another tap, faint this time.

She opened the curtains and at first couldn't see anything but her reflection. She turned off the lamp and looked again. The knocking was coming at a faster pace. When her eyes adjusted, she saw something terrible. Snakes on her window, hitting their heads against the pane, writhing and slithering across the glass. At least a dozen. Savonne jumped away from the window. She watched for a moment as the snakes got bolder and bolder. The light tapping was turning into louder knocking as they struck at the windowpane, again and again. Savonne didn't know what to do. Then she thought of the conjure book. She turned on the lamp, grabbed the conjure book out of her paper bag, pulled the ribbon loose, and flipped to the protection spell. The words looked different now. This time, in her need, she understood what each word meant and how to pronounce them. Protection. She said them out loud in a language she didn't know. A voice in Savonne's brain told her she was speaking French Creole. Haitian. Same as when she summoned the lightning bugs. She didn't know if the words would work without the things listed on the page. She watched as the snakes fell away from the window. All but one. A large one as wide as her arm. She said the words again, but the snake kept knocking its big head hard against the pane.

Savonne ran out of the bedroom and into the kitchen. It was full of people. Black people, all dressed like they just left a funeral.

They turned to her, surprised to see her.

"Who is she?" someone said.

"Snake," she said urgently. "There's a snake after me."

Someone else said, "Is she part of it?"

"There a snake at the window," Savonne said. "It's after me. And the conjure b—"

Savonne remembered. She left the book in the bedroom. If the snake broke through, Diamond John would get the book.

She ran to the foyer and screamed, "Snake!"

Davie appeared at the top of the stairs.

"What the hell?"

"Snake at my window, tryin to break through. I ran out, but I left the... my bag of stuff in there. It's tappin at the window."

"What?"

"A snake is tryin to get in."

Davie trampled down the stairs, did a quick-walk to the bedroom. Savonne followed him. He opened the bedroom door. He could see the window pane move slightly, loosened by the pressure of the snake's body. He saw the snake's big head hit the glass.

"Goddamn!" Davie said. He grabbed the brown paper bag and handed it to Savonne. He backed out, slammed the door closed, and walked Savonne to the kitchen.

"Listen you all," he said to the people filling the kitchen. "Kali's almost finished. She'll be calling you all to go up and see when she's done. She cain't be disturbed when she's in the state that she's in right now. Too dangerous. But we got a problem. This here little girl is being chased by snakes. There's a big snake outside her bedroom window, and I'm gonna go out there and try to kill it. Anybody want to come with me, I'd be mighty grateful."

The people in the kitchen looked stunned. They stood there silent for a moment, taking in what was just told to them. Savonne noticed some of them looked like they were kin. Like they were family. Sisters and brothers and mothers and fathers. All crowded in the big kitchen. All of them dressed in black. Savonne wondered why they were there in the middle of the night.

The man in a three-piece suit took a flask out of his inside jacket pocket and unscrewed the cap. He took a swig, handed the flask to a man that looked very much like him. They had to be brothers.

The man said, "We need fire. That'll scare it away."

The man's brother took a drink and screwed the cap back.

"Yeah, we need some fire and some light to see what we're fighting."

Davie went to the kitchen cupboard and brought out a metal can marked Kerosene.

"Got this," he said and held the can up.

"Got a flashlight?" said the brother of the man in the suit.

"No... But I could drive my car around there, use my headlights to light it up."

Davie went to the foyer and switched on the porch light. He looked over the porch. No snakes.

He took out his car keys. But blocking his car was a line of four cars, parked in a row. Two of them were beat up jalopies. Two of them were newer cars without rust or dents. All four would have to be moved before he could get around to the window, or he'd have to go the long way and circle through the weeds around almost the whole house.

The man in the suit said, "Let me use my car. It's the one at the end. I can get us to the side of the house quicker."

Davie said, "Okay."

"I'm going with you," the other man said.

The three men jogged past the cars to the very last one and got in. Savonne heard the engine start up as she stood watching from inside the door.

The car's headlamps came on and the car jerked in reverse, and then forward toward the side of the house. The man in the suit pulled up to the bedroom window. The headlights shone on a huge snake, a copperhead. Big and wide and at least seven feet long. It was pounding its head on the glass, moving and turning and slithering around the window frame.

"My god," the man in the suit exclaimed. "I ain't never seen nothing like that."

"Me neither," the other man said.

"I got an old blanket in the trunk. We can douse it with your kerosene and catch it on fire. Burn that fucker right off that window."

"Let's do it," Davie answered.

The man got out of the car and popped the trunk. He brought the blanket out and dropped it on the ground. Davie lifted the kerosene can and splashed at the snake. The copperhead lunged at him and, he scuttled away. He poured kerosene over half the blanket, brought out his lighter, and put fire to the edge. It flashed and was flaming and sparking when Davie took it by the unburnt edge and threw it at the window. The blanket caught over the body of the snake and it burst into fire. The snake fell off like an unstuck magnet. Davie followed the snake and poured more kerosene onto it and the flames flashed high. Davie jumped away and went with the two men into the car. They watched as the snake, with the burning blanket partly wrapped around it, writhed and flipped and slithered fast away from the house and into the darkness. The men waited until the snake was gone to the weeds, smoking and flaring a trail of flame. Davie got out of the car, took off his jacket, and beat out the small fire that had started on the wooden window frame.

They backed out of the yard and drove onto the gravel drive. The men went quickly to the front door, looking around for signs of snakes as they walked. Davie and the man in the suit went to Savonne's bedroom and checked the window. The pane was still solid, but tendrils of leftover smoke was seeping through at the edges. Davie closed the bedroom door, and the two walked to the kitchen.

"Never in all my born days have I seen a snake act like that."

"Me neither," Davie said. "I want to thank you for helpin me out."

"Davie?"

Kali was standing at the top of the stairway. Savonne looked up. Kali was covered from head to toe in blood with flicks of matter on her fingers and bits of meat and flesh in her matted hair. She stuck out her tongue and it lolled down like a demon's tongue. The smell of iron, blood, shit, and gall misted down the steps. Sweltered down in a wave of heat.

Frightened, Savonne ran to the kitchen. She felt her stomach flop and acid came up into her throat. Who were these people? Who was Kali? What she been doing upstairs?

"They can come up now," Kali called down.

One by one the family members, some fearful, some eager, moved out of the kitchen and up the stair steps. The man in the suit gave his handkerchief to a small, thin woman wearing a boxy hat. The woman held the handkerchief to her nose. She stopped midway and shook her head, then went down the steps and into the foyer to wait. Davie stayed in the kitchen with Savonne.

"Why is Kali all bloody," Savonne whispered. Her mind was reeling. The events of the last few minutes were bouncing and sparking in her eleven-year old brain. Savonne's eyes welled with tears.

"Why can't I just go home?"

"You will," Davie answered. "We made a promise to your Great-Grandaddy. You'll get home. Safe and sound. Believe me."

"What happened upstairs? Why she so bloody?"

Davie didn't answer for a moment. Savonne watched his face as he formed the answer, taking a minute to decide how much to tell.

Finally, Davie said, "Those people in the kitchen? They here for revenge. A white man, powerful around these parts, killed a young man. A black man. Shot him and threw his body in the river because the young man was in love with the white man's daughter and the daughter was going to run away with the young man."

Davie cleared his throat.

"Those people that went upstairs are the man's family. They pooled their money and paid us to wreak revenge. That's what Kali calls what she does. She wreaks revenge. She's a goddess, come from faraway. Hindu country. She came over here a few years ago for a visit. Now she comes back every now and then, when she's summoned. She's a demon killer. But... she's a little like a demon herself. That white man that killed the young black man? He's no more. Kali tore that man apart. Piece by tiny piece. Nobody ever gonna see that man again."

Davie pulled a cigar out of his breast pocket and lit it.

"Kali's fierce when she gets in her state. Damn fierce. They up there lookin at what they paid for."

Davie winked at Savonne.

"They got their money's worth."

"She ain't gonna do that to me, is she?"

Davie smiled.

"Oh no. Kali weren't sent to hurt you. She's here to protect you. Your Great-Granddaddy made a deal, and me and her, we're here to protect you. Anyways, you ain't done nothin to make Kali want to hurt you. Now, hand me that bucket of chicken. Burnin that snake made me hungry again."

*

Next morning, Kali was all cleaned up and looking like herself. She came down the stairs, wearing her sunglasses, her pearls, and a nice navy polka dot dress with heels to match. She smelled of flowery perfume. Savonne noticed for the first time that the pearls around Kali's neck were little ivory skulls, all strung into a necklace. Kali's skin had changed to the color of a white woman with a buttermilk tan.

As they drove away from the big faded house, down the gravel road, Kali pointed her finger and said, "What's that over there smokin in those weeds?"

Davie slowed the car, looked intently to where Kali was pointing. Thin wisps of smoke were rising from something laying in the weeds. Davie put the car in park, got out, and walked through the weeds toward whatever it was. Savonne got out too. She ran after Davie until they both got to where the smoking thing was laid out. Davie came back to the car, opened the trunk, took out a tire iron, and walked to the thing in the weeds. He handed the tire iron to Savonne.

"Do what you got to do, Vonny," Kali shouted out the car window.

"Do what you got to do," Davie said in a low voice.

Savonne smashed the tire iron hard, down on the smoking thing, raised up and smashed down again and a third time. Davie reached low in the weeds, pulled at something, yanked hard, and brought something up, wrapped his fist around it. He took the tire iron from Savonne, they walked back together, and Davie threw the tire iron in the trunk.

Savonne got into the car. Davie got in the driver's side and before he shifted into gear, he turned to Savonne, handed her a big bloody diamond, and said, "Here you go. Yours to keep."

*

They drove many miles through the humid morning and the hot afternoon. They stopped only for gas or when Savonne or Davie needed to use the toilet. Kali never went to the gas station toilets. She just waited in the car while the attendant pumped the gas or walked in her high heels to the soda pop machine. Savonne wanted to ask why Kali never needed to use the toilet, but she was afraid of what the answer might be.

They let Savonne, who they called Vonny, out of the car right in front of her granny's big house in Indianapolis just around eight o'clock in the evening.

"We don't want to see your granny," Davie said. "We don't want your granny to see us."

Kali sat quiet, smiling like a movie star with a secret, while Savonne pulled the brown paper bag off the seat.

"Nice knowing you, Vonny," Kali said.

"Savonne, my name is Savonne," she answered for the last time.

"Study your conjure book. Learn the spells to protect yourself and your granny," Kali said. "Do that and you be okay. You got the natural in your blood."

Savonne nodded, wide eyed. How'd they know about the conjure book? Did she tell them? Savonne thought back and knew that she did not.

"Now, Davie, let's head out to somewhere I haven't been before."

"Where that be," Davie said. "Shangri La?"

"Been there," Kali said.

"El Dorado?"

"Been there."

"Camelot? Atlantis? Valhalla?"

"Been there, been there, been there."

"Cleveland?"

"Okay, Cleveland."

Davie brought a fresh cigar out of his shirt pocket, put it between his teeth, and lit it.

"You go on in there," Kali said. "Your granny's in there worrying about you."

"Okay."

"We'll wait till you on the porch," Davie said. "So we know we got you from there to here. You remember your granny?"

Kali laughed. "Oh Davie, of course she remembers."

Savonne opened the gate and ran up the steps.

"Okay then. Goodbye," Davie yelled.

Davie put the car in gear and took off. Kali turned in her seat to watch Savonne as they drove away. Savonne looked up at the sky as a bat came bursting out the second story window of the broken-down building next door to Mama Gwen's. The bat circled above her, dipped low, then went high, flapping into the dusk. Savonne wasn't even a little bit scared. She rang the doorbell and waited. Mama Gwen opened the door.

Acknowledgements

Through my years of writing, I sought advice and teachings from the people and organizations I listed below. All of them were wonderful to me and I thank them from the bottom of my heart.

Robert Kent, Andrew Black, Bernadette Bartlett, Richard Winston, Tracy Winston, the Gotham Writers Workshop, the Indiana Writers Center and especially my sister and my greatest supporter, Abbie Winston.

And thanks to my mother, Mary Winston, who instilled in me a never-ending love for art, books, and stories.

Special thanks to Etchings Press for nurturing the sparks and creating the fires.

Colophon

Cover font set in Palantino.
Body font set in PT Serif.

Etchings Press

Etchings Press is a student-run publisher at the University
of Indianapolis. Each year, student editors choose the
Whirling Prize, a post-publication award, in the fall and
coordinate a publication contest for one poetry chapbook,
one prose chapbook, and one novella in the spring. For more
information, please visit etchings.uindy.edu.

Previous winners and publications

Poetry
2019: *As Lovers Always Do* by Marne Wilson
2018: *In the Herald of Improbable Misfortunes*
       by Robert Campbell
2017: *Uncle Harold's Maxwell House Haggadah* by Danny Caine
2016: *Some Animals* by Kelli Allen
2015: *Velocity of Slugs* by Joey Connelly
2014: *Action at a Distance* by Christopher Petruccelli

Prose
2019: *Dissenting Opinion from the Committee for the Beatitudes*
       by Marc J. Sheehan (fiction)
2018: *The Forsaken* by Chad V. Broughman (fiction)
2017: *Unravelings* by Sarah Cheshire (memoir)
2016: *Pathetic* by Shannon McLeod (essays)
2015: *Ologies* by Chelsea Biondolillo (essays)
2014: *Static: Stories* by Frederick Pelzer (fiction)

Novella
2019: *Savonne, Not Vonny* by Robin Lee Lovelace
2018: *Edge of the Known Bus Line* by James R. Gapinski
2017: *The Denialist's Almanac of American Plague and
       Pestilence* by Christopher Mohar
2016: *Followers* by Adam Fleming Petty

Meet the author

Robin Lee Lovelace

Robin Lee Lovelace is the author of numerous short stories that appeared in literary magazines such as *North Atlantic Review, the Crucible, Buffalo Spree* and *Punchnel's*. In 2017, Robin won the grand prize in a one-act play contest, presented by the 30XNinety theatre in Mandeville, a suburb of New Orleans. Robin lives in her home state of Indiana, with her husband and her dog, Amy. She visits her second favorite city, New Orleans, quite often.